WAR

They see the things we can't see....

WATCHERS

WATCHERS

WAR

PETER LERANGIS

AN
APPLE
PAPERBACK

SCHOLASTIC INC.
New York Toronto London Auckland Sydney
Mexico City New Delhi Hong Kong

ISBN 0-590-10999-5

Copyright © 1999 by Peter Lerangis. All rights reserved. Published by Scholastic Inc. SCHOLASTIC and logos are trademarks and/or registered trademarks of Scholastic Inc.

12 11 10 9 8 7 6 5 4 3 2 1   9/9 0 1 2 3 4/0

Printed in the U.S.A.   40
First Scholastic printing, April 1999

WATCHERS
Case File: 6955

Name: Jacob Branford

Age: 14

First contact: 57.34.43

Acceptance:

1

Chronicle of War

May 5, 1864
South of Hobson's Corner, Maryland

I live.
I am one of the lucky few.
The human slaughter has stopped. For now. I have buried fourteen friends. Countless more lie on the battlefield.
I cannot grieve. Nor can I stay idle for long.

Much work must be done. To honor the lost lives. And prepare for the next battle.

It began at dawn. With a noise that sounded and felt like the Earth itself ripping open. My tent mates and I leaped to our feet. Cannon fire. Close.

An unthinkable sound arose in the tent — weeping. "I am only 17!" cried Tom Shelton. "I am too young to die!"

How I <u>hate</u> cowardice. How I wanted to tell him that I am merely <u>14</u>. That I lied about my age in order to fight the good fight. Tom's words were infecting us all with fear and doubt.

Then the first musket blast ripped through the barracks tent and Tom Shelton fell to the dirt. Dead.

And I no longer doubted.

This was war.

I took my musket and ran. Into the blinding rain. Into the line of fire.

"We're behind you, Branford!" shouted one of my men.

The ground was like soup. In the distance, a line of gray Confederate uniforms fouled the ridgeline.

Musket shot flew overhead. I heard the sickening twin sounds of metal with flesh, flesh with mud.

Focus. Concentrate. I fired on the enemy, once, twice.

A gray figure fell limp. Another toppled over the ridge.

I reloaded ten times. Ten vermin killed.

But their numbers were overwhelming, their armaments vast. Bullets and rain vied for dominance of the air.

Glancing behind me, I saw the ground littered with bodies, the blue uniforms darkened by blood.

Alone, I reloaded and fired. Again and again. With each shot, the gray line grew more limp, until finally the attack stopped.

I rushed to minister to my brave, surviving troops.

But I knew the Confederates were not finished. Those I'd left alive were regrouping. I had little time. And only one choice.

I advanced to the ridge. Alone.

My left ear was nearly taken off by a musket shot. The mud, like glue, kept hold of my boots, and I continued barefoot.

As I reached the woods, three Rebel soldiers burst from the undergrowth. A bayonet blade sliced toward my face.

I dodged, then hurtled forward, grabbing one of the men from behind. Holding my dagger to his throat, I ordered the others to disarm.

When the spineless weasels attacked anyway, I

pushed the hostage forward. He met his end at the point of a "friendly" bayonet, but not before I ripped the belt from his waist. With two flicks of the wrist, I lassoed both weapons, flung them away—and then tied up the two others, who were now crying for mercy.

Shouting with blood lust, I ran into the enemy camp. I remember little of what followed — a flying fist meeting an unshaven jaw, a leaping kick connecting to a solar plexus, clanging swords and deadly marksmanship — but my efforts overwhelmed their feeble attempts, and I secured their total surrender!

I returned to camp with a score of prisoners behind me.

There, among my cheering comrades, with an unmistakable expression of admiration, was a man I had only known from portraits, a man up to whose ideal I have patterned my life: the Commander of the Union Army himself, General Ulysses S. Grant.

"Son," he said to me warmly, as he held out a medal of honor, "never in my life have I seen such bravery in the face of almost certain

"**J**ake!"

Jake Branford looked up from his green steno notebook.

It's only Byron. Don't lose the thread. Keep it going. It's good, Jake. It's like you're there.

defeat, he wrote.

"Hello-o-o-o! Welcome to real life, baby brother! Get down here right now!"

"WAIT!" Jake blurted out.

He tried to focus on the page again. *The nineteenth century. The Civil War. Come on, Jake, feel it. FEEL IT.*

Nothing.

The mood was gone.

Jake couldn't write without the mood.

He reached into the open steamer trunk next to him. Lying on top of a pile of old junk was a leather-sheathed dagger and a thread-bare Civil War uniform and cap. Union Army. From the body of one of Jake's ancestors, who died in the war. Or so went the rumor. Mom didn't know for sure. She couldn't care less about stuff like that.

The cap.

Jake put it on. The wool was soft, almost

7

greasy from the years of accumulated grime. It smelled of the past, musty and dark.

From a nearby stack of books he pulled out a slim volume entitled *Nineteenth-century Hobson's Corner: A Photo History*. He flipped it open, scanning the images. Main Street with its ancient-sounding stores — Central Apothecary, Hobson's Corner Dry Goods — the three old brick houses at the top of the hill, the encampment of grim, uncomfortable-looking Civil War soldiers.

In the distance he heard artillery fire. He caught a whiff of campfire smoke and shivered in the morning cool. He felt the grit of gunpowder under his fingernails.

His heart began to slam in a way that never happened during computer games. Or on the playing field. Or even in Civil War "reenactments," where you dressed up and pretended to be in combat, until a car horn spoiled the mood or someone had to leave for a dentist appointment.

Yes.

I've got it.

I'm there.

THIS was real life.

A life where things mattered. Where every day you had something to fight for.

A country on the brink of destroying itself.

A war.

Dirty, loud, sneaky, exhausting.

Totally cool.

You were born at the wrong time, Jake.

Way wrong.

Jake smiled.

Not Jake. Corporal Branford of the Union Army.

He picked up the notebook and pen again. And he began to write.

"WHICH PART OF THE WORD 'NOW' DON'T YOU UNDERSTAND?"

Jake's pen fell to the page.

Gone.

Ripped apart like a canvas tent in a cannon blast.

The mood was over.

Jake slammed the steno notebook shut.

He dug his fingers under the uniform, below the blankets and tablecloths. When he felt the bottom, he pulled at a silken cord, opening a small, empty compartment.

With his other hand, he flipped the notebook so that the cover was faceup:

DO NOT OPEN
If Found, Please Return to
Jake Branford
25 Magnolia Avenue
Hobson's Corner, Maryland 21000
302-555-9072

Then he slipped the book into the hiding
place.

"JAAAAAAAAAKE!"

Jake replaced the cap, let the lid fall shut,
and left the attic.

He resisted the temptation to take the dagger.

The brother?

No, this one.

He has no chance.

He has no choice.

His love for war — it's

Unhealthy.

Fanatical.

But very, very useful.

To whom?

I'm afraid to say.

2

"**W**hat on earth do you *do* up there?" Byron snapped. He was pacing the living room, glancing out the front door. "Never mind. I don't want to know. Just come with me."

"Where?"

"*There*." Byron gestured up the block, where a sports car and a black-windowed limo idled at the curb. Two men and a woman, all wearing sunglasses, stood in front of the cars. "Do you recognize the guy with the gray beard?"

Jake peered out. "Your parole officer?"

"Ha-ha. It's Gideon Kozaar, Jake. *The* Gideon Kozaar? The movie director?"

"Never heard of him. What's he done?"

Byron rolled his eyes. "You were in diapers when he made his last movie. That's his style. Nobody hears about him for years — and then, *boom*, the rumors start: he's making another film. Only no one ever knows for sure, because Kozaar keeps everything about the movie totally secret until opening day. But we know about *this* one — because his casting people were at the high school today, looking for total unknowns. Teens."

"Is *that* what you called me down for? I don't want to be in a movie."

"Not you — me!"

"You can't act! You had two lines in the school play."

"Seven. And you don't *need* experience. He said so. He doesn't even use a script. He just gives the actors a situation and they improvise. Is that easy or what? And if you get cast, you're automatically in the screen actors' union, SAG. Anyway, I had a great audition — but about seventeen million other kids auditioned, too. They can't possibly remember us all. So I have to stand out, Jake. To be different from the rest. You have to help me — "

"Byron?" Jake said, turning back into the house. "Remind me to tell you sometime how much I hate your guts."

"The movie's about the Civil War, dork-face!"

Jake stopped in his tracks.

A Civil War movie? Here?

The feeling.

It was back. Instantly. Right there in the living room.

Careful, you're talking to Byron the truth-challenged.

"I don't believe you," Jake said.

"In the audition they asked us to improvise a Civil War scene. Like we were on the battlefield."

"Where are they filming it?"

"How should I know? It's a secret. Anyway, you're the expert. Tell me how I can impress them — like, dress up in that costume upstairs, go out there and talk in an authentic Civil War accent — ?"

"It's not a costume, it's a *uniform*," Jake said. "And there's no such thing as a Civil War accent."

"So tell me what to do."

Jake went to the door and peered up the block. One of Gideon Kozaar's assistants was pointing to a house and comparing it to a sketch.

"That house wasn't here during the war," Jake murmured.

"So?" Byron snapped.

"So, they're talking about it. Drawing it. Like they're going to use it in the film. And if they do, they'll be wrong."

"That's it. I'll tell them that!"

No.

I will.

"Let's go," Jake said. "I'll do the talking. You just nod and try to look smart. That'll be a perfect acting assignment for you."

He stepped out the front door before Byron could reply.

"Yo!" Jake called out. "That house was built in, like, 1910."

Three pairs of black lenses stared back at Jake. Three bored, annoyed expressions.

16

"You can't say 'hello' first?" Byron whispered, walking behind Jake.

Jake gestured back to his own house. "Ours was here during the Civil War. So were Numbers Thirty-seven, Fifteen, and Fifty-three — except Fifteen didn't have the extra wing."

"Uh, this is my baby brother, Jake," Byron blurted out. "Jake, this is Mr. Kozaar and his talent scouts — "

"Set designers," the woman replied.

"Right. Well, I was just telling Jake about my audition, and — "

"What's the film about?" Jake interrupted. "The Massacre at Standish Crossing? No, wait — the dynamiting of the Underground Railroad near Spencer's Bluff?"

Gideon Kozaar cocked his head toward Jake. His face was wrinkled and thin, his hair brittle and almost white. "I don't know about those," he said in a soft, deep voice.

Jake nodded. "I know. The Battle of Dead Man's Trace, right? Where the Union Army got slaughtered by the Confederates because of their own stupidity. That's the one everyone knows about."

"Oh?" said Gideon Kozaar.

"You don't hear about the others. I have, but I know just about everything about the war. It's like a hobby, I guess — "

"Jake's the history buff in the family," Byron quickly interjected. "I'm the actor."

"My great-great-great grandfather on my mom's side died in the Battle of Dead Man's Trace," Jake barreled on. "Well, supposedly. We don't know his name. People around here have sort of forgotten the details about that battle — even exactly where Dead Man's Trace was. They're still sort of embarrassed about the defeat — which is weird, I know, because it was so long ago, but — "

"So! Uh, would you guys like to *see* our authentic Civil War house?" Byron interrupted.

" — Anyway, to be honest," Jake went on, "in my opinion the Standish Crossing Massacre would be a *much* better idea for a movie than — "

"*Jake!*" Byron snapped. He turned quickly to Gideon Kozaar. "We have antiques and everything. I mean, if you want to do research, hey, this is the place. I can show you around and — "

"Mom said no one's allowed in while she and Dad are in Chicago," Jake said.

Byron glared at him. "She won't mind if Gideon Kozaar visits. So, you guys want coffee and doughnuts?"

The two set designers looked at Gideon Kozaar.

He nodded.

"Great," Byron said. "Jake will get them from the deli."

"What?" Jake protested.

"A dozen assorted. Chocolate cruller for me. Take your time. 'Bye!"

The two set designers followed Byron as he started back toward the house.

"But — but I — "

"I'll give you a ride," rumbled the voice of Gideon Kozaar.

Jake spun around. "You will?"

Gideon Kozaar removed his sunglasses.

Jake's breath caught in his throat.

Silver.

Green.

Yellow.

Kozaar's eyes seemed to be changing color. Slowly, like tinted shades drawn across a window. Jake tried to look away but he couldn't.

"Tell the driver the address," Kozaar said, opening the back door of the limo.

"Hey! Aren't you coming?" Byron shouted.

Jake didn't answer Byron. He felt numb.

He's a stranger.

He's world-famous.

He's creepy.

He's interesting.

And you don't say no to Gideon Kozaar.

"The Corner Pantry," Jake said, climbing into the backseat. "Take a left when you get to Main."

Gideon Kozaar went around and slipped in the other side.

Jake caught a quick glimpse of Byron's bewildered face as the limo pulled away.

Jake swallowed hard and sat back. The car was dead silent. Not even a radio. Gideon Kozaar stared straight ahead.

"Thanks," Jake finally said, "for the ride, I mean — "

"What would you have done?" Gideon Kozaar interrupted.

"Done?"

"At the Battle of Dead Man's Trace. If you were alive then, fighting for the Union."

Good question.

Jake thought a moment. He tried to remember the details of what he'd read. It wasn't much.

"Well, I don't know exactly where it happened," he finally admitted, "or the details of the battle. No one does. But if I were there, and I knew the geography and the Union plans, I would have figured out the ambush. I just know it. And I wouldn't have let the Confederates anywhere near the camp. I would have fought them bare-handed if I had to."

A slow smile spread across Gideon Kozaar's face as the limo began to slow down.

"Here's the Corner Pantry," the driver said.

The car stopped at the curb, and the driver got out to open Jake's door.

"Do you want anything?" Jake asked as he climbed out.

"Yes," Gideon Kozaar said. "But I can wait." Then he gave a signal, and the car drove off.

Byron was pacing the living room alone when Jake got back.

"Delivery!" Jake shouted. "Where is everybody?"

"I can't believe what you did," Byron murmured.

"They left already?" Jake asked.

"You drove away with him. You stole him."

Jake put down his bag on the coffee table, where an old brass oil lamp used to be. "Uh, Byron? Something's missing here."

"I rented it to them."

"Rented?"

"They need props. For the movie. So I showed them around and — "

"Are you crazy? Mom and Dad will kill you!"

"Why? They gave me receipts. They're going to pay us."

"What else did you give them?"

"Nothing. Just some junk from the attic."

The attic.

Jake bolted upstairs.

The door was open. He flicked on the light.

The room felt different. Emptier.

The coat rack.

The old milk can.

Both taken.

He ran into the corner and opened the steamer trunk.

A blanket lay on top, wrinkled.

The uniform, cap, and dagger were gone.

Clever.

As usual, one step ahead of us.

3

"**B**YRON!" Jake shouted.

He flew out of the attic, then stopped short.
The journal.

Jake raced back to the trunk and flipped it open again. He dug his hand to the bottom, yanked on the secret-compartment door, and reached in.

Still there.

He shoved it into his back pocket and bolted downstairs.

"Who said you could give that uniform away, Byron?"

Byron was making faces in the living room mirror. "Is this a good nineteenth-century look?"

"It's from the Civil War! Your great-great-great grandfather wore it!"

"Whoa, hold on, Jake. You *think* he did. No one knows for sure. Mom says it *might* have belonged to him. She doesn't even know his name."

"You had no right!"

"Says who?"

Me.

It's valuable to me.

It connects me. To a place where you'll never go.

To a time I should have been born in.

To a fight. A real one. Bigger than this idiotic argument. Bigger than you or me.

It connects me to a part of myself.

The words formed clearly in Jake's mind. But he didn't say a word.

Byron wouldn't understand.

And Byron was unimportant now.

Only the uniform mattered. The uniform and the cap and the dagger.

Without them, nothing mattered.

Nothing but the present.

And that wasn't enough.

He had to find the stuff and bring it back.

Jake bolted.

"Hey, where are you going?" Byron demanded.

"I don't know."

He let the door slam behind him.

HONNNNNK!

Jake's bike skidded to a stop. His rear tire fanned out, sending up a spray of water.

A red pickup swerved across his path, missing him by inches.

The driver's angry rant was swallowed up by the din of the downpour.

Jake caught his breath, wiping the water from his brow.

The rain had been sudden. It had started when Jake was biking by the Cranfield Mall. Now it was falling so fiercely he could barely see.

Why am I doing this?

No way would Gideon Kozaar be filming in this weather.

Time to cut bait, Jake.

Across the intersection was a steep wooded hill, the southern end of the Menoquan Woods that jutted into Hobson's Corner.

The route home was a long ride around the woods.

The shorter way was straight through. Up and over the hill, through the trees. Muddy but direct. Dangerous, too. Blocked off by a rusted metal fence with NO TRESPASSING signs. No one ever went there, as far as Jake knew.

But the fence had a hole. And Jake was wet. And tired.

He looked up through squinted eyes.

No lightning. It would be safe.

Jake turned his bike toward the hill and began pedaling.

His treads dug in. The soil was wet but packed.

He stood. Pushed.

At the top, the bike slipped. Jake tried to right it. The tires gave out from under him.

Gritting his teeth, he hurtled over the handlebars.

And landed with a thud.

He jumped to his feet, picked up the bike, and looked back down the hill.

Uh-uh. Too slippery.

KAAAA-BOOM!

Great. *Now* it decides to thunder.

No lightning yet.

He pedaled over the top of the hill. Further into the woods.

The path meandered. Split. Split again.

The rain weighed down his eyelashes. The trees melded together in his vision.

Left here. Right. Right.

He was guessing now. Nothing was familiar.

The path petered out, then stopped.

KAAAA-BOOM!

The sky flashed a dull white.

That was close.

Jake let his bike stop. He wiped his brow.

Fog billowed around the pines. To his left and right, the ground seemed to be sloping upward.

The valley.

South of Hobson's Corner, the woods led to a wide valley between two low-lying mountain ranges.

Wrong way, you fool.

Or was it?

He looked for the mountain silhouettes, but the distance was swallowed up in the gathering darkness.

No.

Not all of it.

To his left. A bright patch. The outline of a building.

Shelter.

Jake ran with his bike, tripping over roots, pushing aside branches.

A clearing became visible. Just beyond it, a small hill.

And halfway up the hill, a run-down, wood-shingled hut. Lopsided and windowless. Standing on four stout wooden corner posts.

Jake ditched his bike at the clearing's edge and ran to the hut. The door was secured by a huge rusted padlock. The windows were boarded up.

He slid under the hut, in the space formed by the posts.

The ground was cold but dry. A salamander skittered away, vanishing under a rock.

Jake pulled back his hair. Rivulets of water cascaded down his neck.

Another boom sounded. Loud. Close. Shaking the ground. But this time Jake saw no flash of light.

Weird.

He lay on his stomach and gazed back into the clearing.

A ring of tall pines surrounded the area.

Tall dead pines.

SSSSNNNNNNNNNAPP!

A flash.

An explosion.

A falling tree.

And a shuddering shock wave of heat that seemed to rip across the ground, traveling through the moisture, searing the soil.

Electricity.

It was Jake's last thought before he blacked out.

4

CRACK!
CRACK!
Musket shots.
Ambush.
Man the cannons.
Shoot first, ask questions later.
Don't worry, Colonel Weymouth. I'm here.
You won't lose this time.
You can't.
CRRRRRAAAACKKK!
The sound pierced Jake's consciousness.
Close. Loud.

Too loud.

He jolted upward.

His head smashed against something hard. Wooden.

Ow.

His body ached all over. He felt as if he'd been slammed against a rock. His fingers twitched uncontrollably.

Electrocution.

I should be dead.

With a groan, Jake pulled himself out from under the hut.

He stood on shaky legs and leaned against the wall.

He tried to focus. Blurred, gray-blue images swam before his eyes.

Grass.

Pine trees.

Through their spindly top branches, the sun was attempting to break through.

The rain was now a drizzle. The ground had dried a bit.

A fallen tree lay across the clearing. The tree's stump jutted out of the ground, jagged and white-brown.

A swath of scorched, blackened earth led from the stump to the hut. On a straight line to where Jake had been lying. Like a shadow that had remained after the tree had fallen.

The lightning hit the tree, then traveled toward me through the wet ground.

And I lived.

How much time had passed since then? An afternoon? A week? A year?

Jake glanced at his watch. Three-seventeen. An hour and a half. That was all.

Leave.

Byron doesn't know where you are.

CRACK.

He froze.

The sound again.

The shot.

Not a dream.

Real.

Coming from behind him. From beyond the ridge.

He looked over his shoulder. A puff of bluish-gray smoke rose in the distance.

Go ahead. Just a peek.

He turned, then began to climb.

Toward the top he began hearing voices. A faint whinny of a horse. The clanking of metal. Another shot.

He dropped to his knees and peered over the ridge.

Below him lay a broad valley, dotted with scrub brush. In its midst was a sight that made Jake's jaw drop.

It was a vast encampment with clusters of canvas tents arranged around log cabins. Men swarmed about, carrying crates, grooming horses, cleaning muskets.

Men in blue uniforms.

Dead Man's Trace.

This is it.

The movie set.

To the left, across the valley, a line of soldiers took turns shooting at a metal can on a distant tree stump. Directly below Jake, a group of soldiers sat around a campfire, cleaning muskets. Laughing. Relaxing.

From behind one of the tents a burly guy emerged, wearing a stained white apron and dragging a bloody hunk of meat about three feet long.

"Steak tonight, Cook?" one of the soldiers shouted.

"Last one," the man grunted. "Tomorrow we starve."

Exactly right.

Every detail.

Just like the drawings and photographs.

Better than any Civil War reenactment. Ever.

Jake looked around for cameras. Power lines. Lighting equipment.

Nothing.

Which meant they weren't even shooting film yet. So this had to be a setup. A practice.

Nothing modern to take away from the reality.

Jake grinned.

The feeling.

It was here. Everything — the smells, the sounds, the guts and glory of war.

This was no ordinary movie.

This was perfect.

This was

Heaven.

He stood up. Wide-eyed, he crested the

ridge and began to walk down into the valley.

"HEY!"

A commotion. The men around the camp-fire were scrambling for their weapons.

Amazing.

These actors are incredible.

"Hi!" Jake shouted.

"HALT RIGHT THERE!"

Beyond the men, at the right edge of the camp, a sentry was pointing a musket straight at Jake.

Ask for Kozaar.

Jake dug his hands into his pockets. "Uh, I'm looking for Mr. — "

CRRRRRRRACK!

A puff of smoke.

A whizzing sound.

A sudden loud snap.

"Hey — !"

Jake ducked.

He felt a shower of splinters land in his hair. Behind him, a tree branch had been shot clean off.

Is it — ?

I don't know.

He's not prepared for this.

But the rules . . .

They're not our rules anymore.

This, my friends, is war.

5

Jake stared at the smoking, jagged stub of the branch.

How did they do that?

"Who are you?" a voice called.

"North or South?" asked another.

"Show yourself!"

This is cool.

This is SO cool.

The branch was rigged.

Had to be. A little explosive was strapped to it. Someone set it off by remote control. This is a movie. The gunshot was a blank.

Totally, way unbelievably awesome.

Okay.

Stand up. Play along.

Jake rose slowly. He reached into his pockets, feeling around for something he could use as a white flag. Folded up against his green steno book was a crumpled sheet of loose-leaf paper. A note written to him by his friend Pete.

He waved the sheet and walked down. "I — I come in peace."

But the sentry kept his musket sight trained on Jake. "Who the hell are you?" he growled.

"Jake Branford? Here to see Mr. Kozaar?"

"Ain't nobody here by that name." He cocked the trigger.

Jake jumped at the sound. "Look, I don't — "

"Hold your fire, Harrington!"

An officer was walking toward them briskly from the opposite side of the camp. Scowling. Older than the rest. Heavyset. Thick brush mustache. Big teeth, bucked and grayish-yellow.

Jake held back a laugh.

What do you expect? No orthodontists back then.

Harrington slowly lowered his musket. The other men gathered around Jake, looking at him oddly.

"Where're you from, boy?" asked one of the soldiers, gap-toothed and pock-faced. "The moon?"

Keep. A. Straight. Face.

"Uh . . . Hobson's Corner?" Jake replied.

The officer stood face-to-face with Jake. His brow was lined with sweat. His eyes darted nervously up to the ridge. "Who sent you?"

Jake nearly passed out from the man's breath.

"Mr. Kozaar?" he said, backing away.

"Who?"

"Your director?"

Silence.

Blank, baffled stares. As if Jake were speaking Greek.

And it suddenly dawned on him why he was here.

The real reason.

Duh.

"Is this an audition?" he said. "Because I'm no actor. I just want to get this stuff your set designers took from my house — "

"WHAT ON EARTH ARE YOU TALKING ABOUT?"

Jake stumbled backward at the putrid blast.

They weren't going to give.

Not an inch.

"Okay, I get it!" Jake said. "You can't break character. Cool. I'll *try*, all right? Just give me a minute."

Feel it.

In your bones.

In your soul.

The way it feels in the attic.

You can do it here, easy. Open your eyes. Breathe.

The smell of wood smoke and gunpowder. Of sweat and horse manure. The creaking of wagon wheels and the snap of a holstered pistol against a uniformed leg.

It was all around him.

Not just in his mind.

Jake stood tall. He breathed deep.

He inhaled war.

Yes.

You're where you want to be, Jake.

Where you belong.

And.

You.

Love it.

"Jake — uh, *Jacob* Branford. Reporting for war duty. *Sir!*" Jake shouted.

Two of the men broke out laughing.

"WHO TOLD YOU THIS WAS FUNNY?" the mustached man bellowed.

"No one did, Sergeant Edmonds," muttered one of the men sullenly.

"What's this, Branford?" Sergeant Edmonds suddenly grabbed the note from Jake's hand and peered at it. "'Red button twice for turbo firepower, explode glowing brick to reach nitro depot . . . '?"

Code. For Pete's computer game. "I need that!" Jake said. "It's just . . . code."

"Code?" Sergeant Edmonds began to circle Jake. "How old are you?"

"Fourt — " *You fool. Wrong answer. Too young for the army.* "Fort . . . *Sumter*! What a mistake, huh? Broke my heart. I would have reinforced it more aggressively, *sir*. It was wide open. Biggest insult to the North in the whole war, *sir!*"

"IS SOMETHING WRONG WITH YOUR HEARING? I ASKED YOUR AGE!"

Lie.

"Seventeen!" Jake shot back. "Just thought you might want to hear my fighting experience, sir."

"Fighting experience?" Edmonds leaned closer. Jake held his breath. "Branford, I don't trust you. You're dressed like something from a theatrical show, you sound like a fool, and you're carrying what's either a child's scrawl or secret Rebel code. I'm betting it's the former, so I'll give you a chance. On the condition that Colonel Weymouth agrees with me, after *he* reads it."

"Cool beans." *No no no no.* "I mean, I'll eat *anything* — cool beans, hot beans, whatever." *Concentrate, Jake. FEEL IT.* "Seriously, Sergeant Edmonds, you made the right choice. I can fight with the best of them. Maybe I can help the colonel. I know everything about the war — strategy and tactics and combat and — "

"Just show me you can tie your own shoes and lift a bucket of slops. We'll go one step at a time." Edmonds pointed to a nearby cabin. "Pick up a proper uniform in there and report to me afterward. By then, I'll have talked to the colonel."

Shoulders back, Jake walked to the cabin. He felt ten feet tall.

Yes.

This isn't bad.

It's fun.

But it could be better.

Okay. Plan it out.

Number one. No slang.

Number two. Don't act like a kid.

Number three. Get rid of anything that didn't exist in the 1860s.

Byron will be so *jealous.*

Jake quickly undid his watch and slipped it into his pocket. Then he pulled open the cabin door.

A man barged out, nearly knocking Jake over.

"Whoa. Sorry," Jake said. "Are you, like, the costume guy?"

The man's face was the color and texture of rare roast beef. A scar ran from his left eyebrow to the back of his left ear. Orange-red hair, slick from sweat, stuck out from under his cap.

"Corporal Rademacher to you, lassie."

"Lassie?" *Please.* "I mean, I guess that's authentic, but it is so incredibly sexist — "

SHHHHHINK.

Rademacher drew his dagger. His face was reddening more, his lips drawing back over his teeth. "Are you funnin' me, yard dog?"

Totally deranged.

Jake swallowed.

Don't push him, Jake. You never know.

Lincoln was killed by an actor.

"Uh, no, sir. I — "

"Where are you from, anyway?"

"Hobson's Corner."

"Like hell. What are you doing here?"

"Getting my uniform, that's all — "

Rademacher's voice was a low rasp. "I smell grits on your breath."

"Uh, well, I think it's Cap'n Crunch, but they're both made of corn — " *Cap'n Crunch? Stay in character.*

A flash of steel.

Jake lurched backward.

He felt the cool blade of Rademacher's knife against his cheek.

We've sighted our man.

Then get him. Now. Before he does any more damage.

6

"**D**rop that, Corporal Rademacher!"

Edmonds.

Calling from across the camp.

Jake started to turn.

Pain.

A stinging sensation on his cheek. Sudden. Sharp.

Warm.

He touched his face and felt wetness.

Blood.

His fingers were coated with it.

He cut me.

I'm bleeding.

I'm actually bleeding.

"I can't believe you did that," Jake said.

Rademacher wiped off his dagger and stuck it in its sheath. "It's a U. For Union. Just so everyone knows what side you're on."

"Corporal Rademacher!" Edmonds shouted.

Rademacher's face blanched as he looked toward Edmonds.

Jake turned, pressing his hand to his cheek.

Edmonds was with a woman. She wore a black hoop-skirted dress of thick velvet that swept the ground as she walked. Her hair was dark brown and pulled back in a plain black bow, setting off the silken paleness of her skin and the blue of her eyes. She was staring at Jake with intense concern.

"Are you all right?" she asked, reaching toward Jake's cheek. "What did that barbarian do to you?"

"Mighty sorry, ma'am, I didn't mean it," Rademacher said. "I was cleaning my knife and the boy moved in the wrong direction — "

"You were not cleaning your —" *Yeow.* Talking made the wound bleed even more.

"Isn't anyone helping the boy?" Edmonds asked. "Colonel Weymouth authorized me to let him enlist."

"I'll help him," the woman said.

Rademacher slid by her, smiling sheepishly. "Pardon me, Missus Stoughton . . . Jacob. Dress that wound 'fore it festers, now. Hear?"

As the woman led Jake inside, he could hear Edmonds berating Rademacher outside.

The cabin was dark and crammed full of supplies. Ammunition boxes were stacked head-high against the walls, along with piles of blue uniforms. Jake staggered over toward a canvas chair, his cut dripping a trail of red that streaked across his shirt. He stepped around muskets, bridles, currycombs, feed bags, canvas chairs, benches, old boots, cigar boxes, broken bayonet blades, wagon wheels, and scores of cans, bottles, and crates.

At the other end, three men were sitting on boxes, playing cards on the top of a wooden barrel.

They scrambled to attention when they saw Mrs. Stoughton. Shoving their cards into their pockets, they stepped in front of the barrel and grinned guiltily.

"Which one of you fine gentlemen will be the first to break out of your tableau and locate a dressing for this young man's wound?" Mrs. Stoughton asked.

One of the men scurried across the room, his too-big boots clomping loudly, his thin frame lurching from side to side. He picked up a wooden crate that was marked BANDIGES in childlike handwriting.

Limping back toward Jake and Mrs. Stoughton, he grinned nervously. The few teeth in his mouth were yellow and doomed.

Jake stared at the mouth. *How on earth did they do that?*

Mrs. Stoughton picked the cleanest-looking handkerchief out of the box and began daubing the cut.

"YEOOWWW!" Jake shouted.

"It's not too deep, thank goodness." Mrs. Stoughton moved quickly and efficiently, cleaning the blood and applying a bandage. "I was trained as a nurse. Belle Stoughton is my name. I live in Hobson's Corner."

"Jacob Branford," Jake muttered, moving his jaw as little as possible. "From Hobson's Corner, too."

"Lovely village. I only moved there . . . recently." Mrs. Stoughton's face darkened. "After my dear husband passed away."

A tear trembled on the edge of her eyelid.

Jake felt a tug of sadness.

She's good.

The best actor on the whole set.

"I'm sorry," he murmured.

"Well. I suppose the show must go on, mustn't it?" Mrs. Stoughton forced a smile. "Look here, the bleeding is already easing up. You sit here for a while and keep your head elevated. I must go home now, but Orvis here will change the dressing and give you a uniform while I'm gone."

The skinny, pale, nearly toothless man nodded eagerly.

Mrs. Stoughton stood up and extended her hand to Jake, palm down. "Well, then — "

"Missus Stoughton?" Rademacher was back. He stood in the doorway, cap in hand. His hair had been greased down and he wore a hangdog expression. "Sergeant Edmonds tells me you'll be going home. It would be my pleasure to escort you."

"I won't be needing an escort," Mrs. Stoughton said. "Colonel Weymouth assures me that if our enemies wanted to attack Hobson's Corner, they would have to pass through here first on the way north, so the path couldn't be better protected. If the colonel has faith in my journey, so do I. Good-bye, Jacob, feel better."

With that, she bustled out of the cabin.

"What're *you* staring at, river rat?" Rademacher let loose a hunk of spit that landed between Jake and Orvis. Then he stomped away.

"I think spit is meant for me." Orvis pulled off Jake's bandage and cleaned his skin with a moist towel.

"He's out of control," Jake said. "Ow."

"Try not to talk. Corporal not bad. Heart-broken, is why he like this."

Bizarre accent. Jake couldn't place it.

"What did you say?" Jake asked.

"Corporal lo-o-o-ove the Widow Stoughton. Courted her. Bring her to here. Is big mistake. Introduce her to the colonel. Colonel wife dead, he need lady friend. Widow Stoughton husband dead, she need man friend. They fall in love. Corporal heart, *ccchhhhh*. Broke. He never happy after that. Still love her."

Jake exhaled. "Okay, can I take a time-out — I mean, from acting?"

Orvis cocked his head.

"There's a big difference between the two actors," Jake continued. "The one playing Mrs. Stoughton? She's full of sadness and emotions and all. I can *feel* it. But the Rademacher guy? I mean, I'm not an actor, but even I know you can *act* violent without *being* violent. Isn't there a rule against that, anyway? In SAG or whatever?"

"Sag?"

"The screen actors' union? Isn't it — *oh, come on*! Don't you guys ever let up? Even for a *stab wound*?"

"Cut is not serious. Orvis taking good care of it!" He moved closer to Jake, lowering his voice to a whisper. "I say something personal? You no talk like others."

"No? I'm trying!"

"You Rebel?"

"Huh?"

"Hey, Orvis!" yelled one of the other men. "Are you in?"

"Ja!" Orvis looked anxiously over his shoulder at the men, who were settling into their card game again. Then, with a wink at Jake, he whispered, "Go. Take uniform from pile. But remember — after war, Orvis go to side that wins. All work is good, no? *Even pick cotton.*"

With that, he limped back to the game.

What was that all about?

No time to wonder.

The uniform pile — *that* was where the attic uniform might be.

Jake quickly rummaged through.

Too new . . . too ripped-up . . . too small . . .

No luck.

Dejectedly, Jake picked out a uniform roughly his own size. It was itchy and smelled of horse and smoke, but it fit. He slipped on a pair of stiff, clumsy boots. Carefully, he transferred his watch, money, and steno notebook into the pants pockets.

"BRANFORD!" Sergeant Edmonds's voice boomed from outside the cabin.

Jake ran out. "Yes, sir!"

The cut on his cheek stung. He held the bandage tightly against it.

Edmonds was standing by a nearby tent, talking to a group of soldiers. "Jacob Branford, the colonel may have accepted you, but I have my doubts. It seems these other gentlemen are all from Hobson's Corner. But not a one of them recognizes you."

"Well — I — I — " *It's acting, Jake. Act!* "My family's new in town, sir. And people don't know us too well. I'd be happy to show you where I live if — "

"Fine. Good idea. Colonel Weymouth wants me to send a party into the village for supplies, anyway," Edmonds said. "I strongly suggest you join these men and direct them to your house."

That was easy. Too easy.

Jake swallowed hard.

They were agreeing to take him home. But once they were there, the audition would be over.

No.

Wait. I was just getting the hang of this.

I haven't had a chance. I was just warming up. They think I'm terrible. But I can be better.

Now what? "Bye-bye, don't call us, we'll call you"?

Jake looked at Edmonds's eyes for a sign. A wink or a glimmer of kindness — anything.

But all he saw was fatigue and hostility.

Tell me!

Am I in or out?

Didn't these guys know how this felt? They were *actors*, for god's sake, they should have some sympathy.

It was only a movie. But he knew it was the closest he would ever get to the real thing. To a real war.

He'd had a taste. And he wasn't going to give up easily.

Show them. In the time you have left, be great.

Jake saluted crisply. "Yes, sir, Sergeant Edmonds! I'll lead the way!"

Edmonds turned away. "The men leave tomorrow. At dawn."

"Tomorrow?" Jake shot back. "I have to stay here *overnight*?"

"Is that a problem?" Edmonds said. "Do you need someone to tell you a bedtime story?"

Stifle it, Jake. This is good. They're giving you more time!

"No, sir!" Jake snapped. "Dawn tomorrow!"

Edmonds walked away. The other soldiers stood shoulder to shoulder, hands resting on their weapons.

"We are your tent mates," said a broad-shouldered man with a crooked nose. "I'm Schroeder, and this here's Platt."

Next to him, a scraggly bearded man cackled. "You're welcome to try to escape. I wish you would."

"Platt is a sharpshooter," Schroeder explained. "He will wait until you reach the bottom of the hill. He will let you climb to the top. And just as you're about to disappear, just as you think you've made it, he'll turn his back, hold up a mirror, and shoot."

BLAM!

With the slightest glance to the left, Platt took a shot.

Clear across the camp, the can on the tree stump exploded into shards.

"And you, my friend, will be a dead man."

Did you make contact?

Yes. But he slipped away.

What happened?

He said he needed to teach a lesson.

A *lesson?*

1

"**O**hhhhhh . . ."

The rising sun hurt Jake's eyes, even through the thick canvas of his tent. He hadn't slept all night.

For one thing, his cheek hurt. The congealed blood on the bandage made it stick to his skin.

What's more, the tent smelled ten times worse than the Hobson's Corner Regional Middle School gym locker room. And he was fairly certain his bedding had fleas.

He stood up from his hay mattress, scratching like crazy. His two other tent mates were silently putting on their uniforms. Schroeder spat loudly on the floor. Platt picked nits from his hair.

"Guys, is there any bug spray?" Jake blurted out.

Schroeder ignored the question. "Who's Kozaar?" he asked.

"Kozaar?" Jake repeated.

"And Byron," Platt said. "You said the names in your sleep. Colonel Caleb Byron of the Confederates, mebbe? Does he unnerstand your secret code?"

"He's my brother!" The fleas were killing Jake. He pulled on his uniform. Raced outside. Breathed in some fresh air. Scratched.

A hand landed on his shoulder. Schroeder's. "If you're planning on going, better do it now. You got Platt all excited."

Jake spun around. Platt was lifting his musket.

"Look, I need a new bandage," Jake said. "And I think I have fleas. So — "

Schroeder grabbed him by the collar and began to drag him.

Another soldier was walking by, toting two

buckets of water. Schroeder grabbed one of the buckets, set it on a rock pile, and shoved Jake's face into it.

Jake struggled for breath. Ten seconds. Twenty.

Then up.

"GAHHHHH!" Jake coughed and spat, gulping in air.

Around him, a group had gathered. They were guffawing. Pointing.

The bandage was floating in the water, now pink-red.

Take the pain.

Deal with it.

"Shall we work on those fleas?" Schroeder asked.

"No thanks!" Jake blurted out.

Schroeder pushed him roughly through the gawkers. "Then let's go."

They headed toward the ridge. Soon six of the men fell into lines on either side of him.

Jake felt the butt of a musket in his back.

Platt. Pulling up the rear.

Jake stumbled forward, sandwiched among the eight men. Edmonds's men.

Like a prisoner.

He rubbed his cheek.

Sore. But not too bloody. The water seemed to have done it some good.

At the base of the ridge, they followed a narrow trail that led upward through the scrub brush.

Jake eyed the top, trying to spot where he'd come over the day before.

There.

He looked for the hut. No luck. The forest was too dense.

"Move!" Platt ordered.

Jake felt the musket in his back again. Harder.

SMMMMMACK!

One of the men swatted Platt's weapon away with his own musket. "The boy can move on his own."

The stranger's hair was reddish-brown, like Jake's. His face was intelligent and strong. Of all the men, he was the only one who looked as if he'd shaved or brushed his teeth during the last week.

And the only one with a hint of kindness in his eyes.

"Thanks," Jake said softly. "I'm Jake Branford."

"Jedidiah Samuelson," the man replied. "Way I see it, you're our guest, not our prisoner. So far."

They were trudging over the crest now. Into the woods.

"All right, Hobson's Corner lad," Schroeder said. "You lead us."

Oh, great.

Just fantastic.

You stay out of the stupid woods your whole life. And now that you have to find your home, now what?

He looked around for some familiar road. Some sign.

Nada.

Just a few barely worn paths.

Eeny, meeny, miney, mo.

"Okay, follow me," he said, heading for the path to his right.

Platt ran around to the front of him. He was grinning. "Reckon you don't know your north from your south."

Samuelson nudged him gently to the left.

"I meant, *that* way," Jake said.

The men formed around him again. And they began a long, silent march.

Maybe it was the itching, or the pain in his cheek, or the ill-fitting boots, but by the time the houses came in sight, Jake was cranky and exhausted.

The trip had seemed long. Too long.

They're actors. They don't know the woods, either.

We probably went clear up to Delaware and back.

But he was home.

Finally.

And Byron and his parents would find out everything.

If they didn't know already.

If Kozaar hadn't already contacted them.

Quiet.

The village was too quiet.

No car noise. No lawn mowers. No nothing.

Which made no sense. They were approaching School Street, near the big playground —

Dirt.

The road was unpaved.

Jake looked around, bewildered.

They'd reached a village, all right.

But it wasn't Hobson's Corner.

No streetlights. No playground. No water tower in the distance, or Kmart down the road, or World War II statue at the corner of School and Main, which would be right there —

His thoughts suddenly stopped.

He tried to say something, but no words came out.

At the nearest corner to the left, where the dirt road intersected a cobblestone street, a granite post was carved with the names SCHOOL ST. and MAIN ST.

Exactly where it should be.

Just up Main Street was a medium-size clapboard house.

The museum. The Overmyer Memorial Museum. Left to Hobson's Corner by one of its founding families.

But it was different.

Smaller. Missing the porch and the addition on the back.

Not to mention the brass sign on the front lawn. And the dogwood trees. And the ramp leading to the front door.

And in the first-floor window, where the front office should have been, Jake could see . . . *furniture*. No file cabinets. No computer terminals.

"They're supposed to be here still," muttered one of the soldiers, a worried-looking man with flaming red hair and freckles. He began running toward the house. "Mama? Papa?"

"Where are you going?" Schroeder thundered.

"My house!" the man shouted over his shoulder.

"Overmyer, get back here!"

Is he — ?

Did they — ?

Reestablish contact immediately!

8

*R*idiculous.

Impossible.

But they were walking down a street called Main. With a curve just like the one in Hobson's Corner. And cobblestones, like the ones that peeked through the worn-out blacktop back home.

But the blacktop was gone. The sidewalks were made of brick, not cement.

And the buildings were different.

Smith's Eatery. A blacksmith shop.

The Pottery Shack. Now Central Apothecary.

Ben's Hardware. Hobson's Corner Dry Goods.

And just above Main Street, before it angled out of sight, were three brick houses. The ones Mom always dreamed of living in.

They were different, too.

Unpainted. Unlandscaped.

But the same.

The same as

The book.

That was it. The book in the attic. *Nineteenth-century Hobson's Corner: A Photo History*.

Jake glanced back at the shops on Main Street. Squinted. Tried to frame the image. To imagine it in black-and-white. With specks of dust. Scratches.

Yes.

That was it.

The shape of the buildings. The texture of the street.

Just like the photos.

Main Street, Hobson's Corner, in the 1860s.

But how?
How can I be here?
How can I be in
The
The
He rewound the last twenty-four hours in his mind. Back to the bike trip through the woods in the rain.

To the hut.

And the
Lightning.
I was hit by lightning.
My brain was scrambled. I'm imagining this.
Or worse.
Maybe I'm not here at all.
Maybe I'm
I'm
No.
Don't even think of it.
Was this what it felt like to be dead?

He didn't feel dead at all.

Just the opposite.

He felt reborn.

Alive.

Totally alive.

As if he were finally, for the first time in his life, home.

Okay. Okay. Calm down, Jake. Think.

They built a replica of the Titanic. *They could have built Hobson's Corner, too.*

Silently. Without anyone finding out. A whole village built in total secrecy.

It was possible. Maybe.

But maybe not.

Platt was walking up the street now, poking open some doors, kicking open others.

"Where is everybody?" Jake asked.

"You should know," Schroeder said acidly. "You live here."

Cedarville. Remember your history, Branford.

Of course. The people in Hobson's Corner were evacuated to Cedarville right before the battle, in case the Rebels attacked. Only a handful of people stayed behind. But where were they?

"I — I meant the ones who didn't go to Cedarville," Jake said.

"Nobody," Platt called out. "Anywhere."

"If they left, they would have told us," said one of the men.

"Unless the Rebels came in and got 'em," said another.

"From where?" Schroeder snapped. "Our camp is smack in the middle of their only access route. Are you suggesting the Rebels went two hundred extra miles, around the mountain, then doubled back? Because that's what they'd have to do."

"They would do it," Platt said, "if they knew where we was. And jus' maybe they'd send ahead a small, innocent-looking spy to our camp."

The men fell silent.

And they all looked at Jake.

Jake gulped. "Whoa, guys, don't jump to conclusions. I'm —"

"— in big trouble," Schroeder said. "Colonel Weymouth is not kind to soldiers who break his trust. Platt, you and Williams check the Cedarville Road. Morris and Johnson, you check across Pine Street, down to the field —"

"What about the boy?" Platt asked.

"I'll go with him," Samuelson volunteered.

"Find where he *says* he lives," Schroeder said, rushing off. "And if he's lying, take care of him."

Samuelson pushed Jake toward School Street. The other men started off, grimly clutching their muskets.

"Wait!" Jake protested. "That's unfair! You wouldn't — "

"Just show me your house," Samuelson whispered.

"Okay, okay." Jake tried to collect his whirling thoughts. "But I'll tell you right now, my family's not going to be there."

Samuelson nodded grimly. "Of course not. They're in Cedarville."

"But — Schroeder said — "

"Schroeder and Platt belong in a cage," Samuelson grumbled. "I know you're not a spy. The Rebels have been reading us for some time now. We all sense it. Sniper fire, stolen plans, strange noises at night — they've been going on for days. And if you ask me, Weymouth's strategies leave us wide open. No, if there *is* a spy, he's been among us — he wasn't sent ahead only now. They need an outsider to blame. They're grasping at straws. You came along at the wrong time, Jake."

Samuelson fell silent. When he and Jake reached School Street, they turned left.

They passed a tiny wooden shack. Beyond it was a cornfield.

Where the middle school and football field should have been.

The road went straight . . . past Sycamore Street, Linden . . .

Spruce.

Jake shivered. The path felt so familiar under his feet. But the houses, the trees . . .

Home.

There it was.

Jake couldn't breathe.

In front of the house was a huge scraggly yard. A shack where the garage should have been.

No screen door. No bay window.

The door hung open, swaying in the breeze.

"Want to look inside?" Samuelson asked softly.

Jake barely heard him. He was walking through the front door. Looking.

Plain dark-wood chairs sat stiffly in the living room. The floors were bare and wooden, covered only by old oval rag rugs. The kitchen was simple — cupboards, basin, counter.

Only the shape was the same. The frame. The dimensions . . .

It was his house. He knew it in his bones.

He walked from room to room, under the lintels he knew so well, the ceilings that were a little too short because the people were so much smaller then.

Not then.

Now.

A sudden boom snapped Jake out of his reverie.

Thunder?

Jake looked around for Samuelson.

He walked to the kitchen. He could see the sky through the window — clear, sunny —

A shout.

From the backyard.

CRRRRACK!

That wasn't thunder.

He ran to the back door and threw it open.

Samuelson lay on the grass. Bleeding.

Just beyond him, in the woods, was a group of men.

Dozens of them.

Armed.

And dressed in gray.

Rebels.

Theirs.

9

"**N**o!"

Jake grabbed Samuelson's arm and tried to drag him inside.

"Save yourself, Jake," Samuelson rasped. "Leave . . . me."

Jake heard the clomping footsteps. He turned.

A Confederate officer loomed over him. A barrel-chested man with a pockmarked face and long, stringy black hair.

"We don't kill the small fish," he said. "Just the full-grown ones. So back off."

He dug the butt of his musket into Jake's chest and pushed him aside.

Then he took aim at Samuelson.

"Don't shoot him!" Jake leaped at the man.

He stepped back, grinning. "Brave little fella. Okay, have it your way. *You* kneel down, nice and easy, and give me all your big brother's weaponry. Then I want you to yell your little head off. Just in case your friends haven't heard us yet. Lure the big fish to us."

Jake glanced uneasily at Samuelson. "What'll you do to him?"

"JUST DO IT!"

Samuelson nodded. Gestured toward his musket.

Jake knelt beside him.

Grab it.

Shoot them.

Put them out of their misery.

"Do . . . exactly what they want," Samuelson said, his voice barely a whisper.

Jake slowly removed Samuelson's musket and dagger. They were both much heavier than he expected.

The Rebel officer was aiming at Jake now.

Jake stood. He approached the man, holding out the weapons.

SMMMACK!

The door.

Jake looked over his shoulder.

A face.

Red hair.

Overmyer.

In the kitchen doorway. Staring at Jake. At the weapons. At Samuelson.

"What the — ?"

A shot interrupted his sentence.

Overmyer dived back into the house. The kitchen window exploded in a hailstorm of glass.

"FI-I-I-I-IRE!" shouted the Rebel leader.

CRRRACK!

CRRRACK! CRRRACK! CRRRACK!

No time to think.

Jake pulled Samuelson into the house. Shoved him into the kitchen.

Overmyer was slumped over a basin, eyes closed.

Shouts. Behind them, inside and outside the house.

Platt. Schroeder. Morris. Williams. Johnson.

KA-BOOOOM!

The house next door. Jake could see it out the side window. Collapsing inward.

"They have cannons!" shouted Schroeder.

Cannons?

Jake leaped toward Overmyer.

He was breathing. But unconscious.

Jake grabbed his musket. Felt its weight.

Its power.

The feeling.

Jake's body was coiled. His teeth clenched.

Do it, Jake.

Just do it.

He ran to the back window. Fell to his knees. Took aim.

Fired.

Click.

Nothing.

CRRRRACK!

The window above him shattered.

"Get down, you fool!"

It was Schroeder.

He pulled Jake to the floor.

"AAAAAAGGHHHHH!"

Platt was running through the house now.

Toward the back door, musket drawn. His face was crimson, his eyes the size of base-balls.

Deranged.

"NO-O-O!" Schroeder yelled.

"THEY KILLED JOHNNNNSONNNNNN . . ." Platt yelled.

He sprinted into the backyard, firing into the trees.

At least three Rebels fell. Two more rushed Platt from either side, aiming their muskets at him.

Platt ducked. The shots crossed over his body. The two men lurched into the air, then fell to the ground, each the other man's victim.

Jake cringed.

With a deafening *BOOM*, a nearby tree burst into flames.

"RETREAT!" shouted Schroeder. "We're out-numbered!"

Morris headed for the front door.

Schroeder lifted Overmyer.

Jake linked his arm around Samuelson's shoulders. But Samuelson was limp.

"That's . . . him!" Overmyer was pointing to Jake. His motions were feeble but his eyes sharp and accusing. "I saw him helping the Rebels. That's the spy!"

They're playing right into his hand.

10

"It was a misunderstanding," Jake insisted. They were in the woods now. Almost to the camp. He and Harrington were struggling to drag Samuelson over the path. "When Samuelson comes to, he'll tell you — "

"WHO ASKED YOU TO SPEAK?" shouted Schroeder from behind him.

Any minute Jake expected the Rebels to fire. The escape from Hobson's Corner had been slow going. Samuelson was unconscious and heavy. The others had gone on ahead to prepare the encampment for attack.

But now they were approaching the ridge, and the Rebels hadn't followed.

The camp was in pandemonium. As they carefully moved Samuelson down the path, men were shouting instructions, loading muskets, bridling horses, shouting the news.

Jake heard the same phrases over and over: one dead . . . two injured . . . town empty . . . don't know how they got past . . . must have been tipped off . . . didn't follow us . . . don't know why.

Jake knew why.

They're moving in from both sides now.

They have us just where they want us.

When they've gathered themselves within striking range, we're dead.

Now Orvis was rushing out of the supply cabin. "Is he . . . ?" he called out.

"Not yet," Jake replied.

"I help." Orvis nudged Jake aside, putting his arm around Samuelson.

Suddenly Jake felt a hand grabbing the back of his collar. "This way, swamp rat."

Platt.

Jake tried to protest, but Platt was pulling him across the camp, weaving through the panicked throng — and right into Edmonds's tent.

"Just try to escape," Platt said, gripping his gun. "You'll make me and my blunderbuss very happy."

"You need me out there," Jake insisted. "I can help!"

"The way you helped at Hobson's Corner? The way you set us up? Why, I'd shoot you right here if'n Edmonds didn't say to keep you for him."

With that, Platt turned away and stood at attention, keeping sentry.

Jake straightened his collar. The tent was large. No people. Just a table in the center, covered with a map.

Jake moved closer.

The map showed two long mountain ranges with a wide pass between them. In the pass was a big red circle. *The camp.*

At the top of the map — north — the pass became a forest that eventually ended at a village, marked by crudely drawn houses and a church. *Hobson's Corner.*

From the south, large black arrows labeled with the word REBELS pointed into the pass.

From the camp, blue arrows pointing south. Edmonds's plan of attack.

No post in the mountains. No guard watch to the east or west. No reconnaissance.

This was amateurish.

Stupid.

Hobson's Corner was wide open to a sneak attack.

No wonder the Confederates got through.

What was he thinking?

"You left him in there ALONE?" thundered Edmonds's voice.

Jake spun around.

Edmonds was barging into the tent. Wild-eyed, drenched with sweat. He pushed Jake aside and grabbed the plans off the table.

"Sergeant Edmonds," Jake said. "I can explain — "

BLAAAAM!

They both turned.

Now Corporal Rademacher was storming inside, his pistol smoking.

Only Platt's legs were visible. Flat on the ground. Platt was howling with pain.

Rademacher shot him.

"You trigger-happy fool!" Edmonds said.

Rademacher pointed his pistol at Jake. "He let that schoolboy Rebel in here. And I aim not to let him out!"

No.

Jake backed away. "I'm not a spy! I can help you!"

"RADEMACHER!"

A deep voice. A new one.

Rademacher froze. He lowered his gun, cursing under his breath.

Jake recognized the man who now came through the tent flap. He'd seen the man's cracked, faded photo in books — the droopy, walruslike white mustache, the fierce blue eyes and deep-lined skin, the broad shoulders and ample belly.

Weymouth.

"Colonel, our men have identified this boy as the spy," Edmonds said. "Overmyer saw him aiding the Rebels, looting Samuelson's body while he was still alive."

Jake felt impaled by Weymouth's cold, steely eyes.

"I — I was at gunpoint!" Jake pleaded.

"They ordered me to take the weapons. Then they wanted me to shout, so the rest of the guys would come into the trap. That was when Overmyer showed up. *That's* what he saw."

"Liar!" Rademacher shouted.

Colonel Weymouth came face-to-face with Jake. *"Would* you have shouted if Overmyer hadn't come?"

"Well — I — "

Yes.

I would have.

Probably.

"My life was in danger," Jake said softly.

Edmonds was fuming. "So you'd risk the lives of the other men."

"Treacherous pond scum — " Rademacher lunged forward.

Colonel Weymouth turned his head, and Rademacher stopped in his tracks.

"Gentlemen, we have bigger concerns right now," Weymouth said. "We will keep the young man in the compound jail until we have rid the countryside of our Southern nemesis. Then, if we are still alive, we will conduct a fair trial — "

"Jail?" Jake blurted out. *Impossible. Not during a great battle.* "What am I going to do there? I won't be able to fight!"

"And Corporal Rademacher here will be your guard," Weymouth went on. "Judging from the way he treated Mr. Platt, he's having a bit of trouble discerning who the enemy is — so we will keep him away from battle."

Rademacher's face fell. "But — but sir — "

Colonel Weymouth ignored him and addressed Jake. "You will, of course, be able to present your case — eyewitnesses and so forth."

"I don't have any eyewitnesses!" Jake replied.

"Just tell us what you know about the Rebels," Edmonds snapped.

"I DON'T KNOW ANYTHING!"

"A shame." Colonel Weymouth raised a heavy white eyebrow. "That kind of statement tends not to work well in a court-martial proceeding."

Court-martial.

Trial by military officers.

Weymouth, Rademacher, and Edmonds.

103

I don't stand a chance.

"But what if I lose?" Jake asked. "Doesn't someone have to, like, *shoot* me?"

"No, no, no." Rademacher smirked. "Not *someone*. A firing squad."

Jail?

Firing squad.

Excuse me. Contact reestablished. We got him back.

And?

He told us to mind our own business.

11

"String 'im up, that's what they're gonna do — even though he's a boy. Just to make an example."

BOOOM!

"Shame, ain't it, Clarence? They blame the weakest ones. The place is crawlin' with *real* moles, but they'll never get caught."

Crrrack! Crrrack! Crrrack! Crrrack!

Jake jumped at the shots.

That'll be me.

Before the firing squad.

Blindfolded.

Hands tied.

One last request, kid. What'll it be?

What *would* it be? To see Mom?

This wasn't fun.

Seeing Johnson die. Watching Samuelson bleed from a wound. Hearing Platt scream from a point-blank shot. Looking up the barrel of a loaded musket.

Special effects?

No. It's too real. Death can't be faked like that. Another person's pain can't feel so nauseating if it's just acting.

The feeling was gone now. The way he imagined war, up in the attic —

It's nothing like that.

Nothing.

"If they had half a brain," said the first man, Clarence, "they'd put that snake Orvis in here, too."

"A *full* brain, and they'd get Rademacher."

From inside the cabin, Rademacher's voice called out, "Shut your mouths, 'fore I pump 'em full of buckshot!"

Clarence lowered his voice to a whisper. "He's got the curse, Jamie. The anger. Makes him blind. He shot Platt."

"That don't mean he'd turn sides."

"He would, for revenge. The Colonel stole his girl. Plumb destroyed him."

"Aaaah, Rademacher don't do nothing less'n Edmonds tells him."

"So who says ol' Edmonds ain't in on it, too?"

"Hey — maybe all of 'em are!"

Both men burst out cackling.

Enough.

"Stop it!" Jake shouted. "How can you guys stand it in here? How can you *laugh?*"

"Don't know what you're complaining about, fella." Clarence jerked a thumb out the window. *"They're* the ones fightin'. We got it easy in here."

"Don't you *want* to fight?" Jake asked. "Isn't that why you enlisted?"

"Hoooo-hahaha! That's good!" roared Jamie. "I came here 'cause they would've arrested me back home."

"I came here 'cause I was paid to," Clarence said. "That's how it works. A rich gen'leman can avoid service by sending a paid fella like me in his place."

Hopeless idiots.

109

"But — but — this is the greatest war of all time," Jake said. "The whole country is falling apart — and *you* can fight it. Destroy the enemy. Show them who's boss — "

"Yeeee-hahh!" Jamie whooped. "We'll just watch *you* do it!"

Cowards.

They were the lowest forms of life Jake had met.

Even their opinions were stupid.

Orvis, a spy?

Jake remembered what Orvis had said when he'd first met him — "You Rebel?"

He was the one who first suspected me.

Edmonds? Rademacher?

Ridiculous.

Absolutely off the wall.

It had to be someone else. Someone suspicious. Someone who left clues. Like . . .

Like . . .

Jake sat on the cell's one chair. His mind was numb. Images began bubbling up.

Like Orvis. Hinting he wanted to go south. To work.

What did that mean? Was it a signal? Was

he testing my response to see if I was a Rebel?

Or . . . is he one himself?

Like Edmonds, with his battle plan.

Incompetent beyond belief. As if he wanted the Confederates to win.

Like Rademacher and his temper. The way he casually shot Platt.

Revenge? Sabotage? Wouldn't put it past that dude.

Maybe they *were* working together.

Maybe Clarence and Jamie weren't so crazy.

FOOOOOOOM!

The ground shook violently. Jake and his two cell mates fell to the dirt.

"Uh-oh, that was from the north," Clarence remarked.

"Ohhh, we're gon' get it now!" Jamie shouted.

The north.

The direction of Hobson's Corner.

The Rebels were closing in now. From both sides.

Like . . .

"Pincers," Jake said.

"Say *what*?" Jamie asked.

Pincers. A squeeze. Two-sided advance. Solution: Blast enemy with heavy artillery during daylight. Keep them at bay while conserving as much musket ammo as possible. Fan out into the mountainside under cover of darkness. Next morning, enemy ambushes empty camp. Soldiers fire from hidden outposts in counterambush.

Jake remembered the strategy. From a book. Some Civil War battle.

A Union victory. Against all odds.

CRRRACK! CRRRACK! CRRRACK! CRRRACK!

A bullet flew through the cell window. Jake, Clarence, and Jamie flattened themselves.

Get the plan to Weymouth before it's too late!

"I know what to do!" Jake shouted. "I know how to win this!"

"Better hurry," Jamie remarked. " 'Cause we ain't got long."

Jake pulled out his green steno book and began to write.

Green? Did they have green paper then?

Or wire-bound notebooks?

DOES IT MATTER?

Move to reopen contact. We don't have much time.

He's blocking channel one.

Trying two . . .

12

"Early letter to Santy Claus?" asked Clarence, peering over Jake's shoulder. "Would you like me to run it to the mailbox?"

No time to waste. Don't talk.

Jake scribbled as fast as he could, letting the two men look on.

He drew a map — the pass, the mountains, the village. He drew the enemy position, closing in.

And he drew the battle plan — a series of arrows and a brief explanation underneath.

The picture was crude, but the words would explain everything.

Military Tactics for Beginners. I can't believe they haven't thought of this themselves.

"It's a map," Jamie whispered.

"Well, I'll be . . ." Clarence murmured.

"They was right," Jamie said.

Now both men were backing away toward the cell door.

Jake glanced up. *"Who* was right?"

"You're the one," Jamie said. "You're the — "

Clarence began banging on the cell bars, shouting at the top of his lungs. "Hey! GUARD! RADEMACHER!"

Rademacher stormed in. "Shut your mouth 'fore I — "

"He's the spy!" Clarence said, pointing at Jake. "It ain't us! He's making plans for the Rebels! We caught him!"

"What are you talking about?" Jake said. "Didn't you read the explana — ?"

Jake cut himself off. The two men were staring at him, their eyes fearful, hopeful, and vacant.

No.

They didn't read it.

They can't read.

Of course. It was the 1860s. Not everybody was literate. Not everybody went to school.

"I can explain!" Jake said.

"I'm sure you can." Rademacher was grinning. "What's on that itty-bitty piece of paper you're holding?"

"A battle plan — for us! I know how we can win — "

Fool.

Don't give it away.

Not to him.

You can't trust him.

Jake held the paper behind his back. "I demand to see Colonel Weymouth at once!"

"Funny, I thought *I* was the one who made demands around here." With one swift move, Rademacher reached between the cell bars and grabbed the paper from Jake's hand.

"NO!"

Rademacher made a big show of reading the map — scratching his chin, tapping his jaw. "Hmm, looks mighty interesting. Why, I'll be sure to give it to him myself. Y'all behave while I'm gone, Southern boy, hear?"

With a sneer, he folded the map and left the cabin.

Jake slumped against the wall, glaring at Clarence. "You ruined it. You destroyed our chances."

"Sorry, kid," Clarence said. "It's a war. A man's got to do what a man's got to do."

Suddenly new memories were bubbling up. Stuff he'd read long ago about the Battle of Dead Man's Trace.

This is how they lost.

The Rebels knew the Union Army's every move. They anticipated the counterstrategies. Their spies infiltrated the ranks.

They blew the Federals to smithereens.

I could have stopped it. But I didn't.

I gave it away.

He gazed out the window. At the encampment.

No. Not the encampment anymore. The battlefield.

The killing field.

Rademacher was running, hunched down, eyes peeled, the green paper still in his right hand.

Near Colonel Weymouth's tent, he ducked

behind a fortification of sandbags. He was scanning the note now, reading it. Orvis was limping past him, his arms full of first-aid supplies.

Suddenly Rademacher grabbed Orvis by the arm and shouted something that Jake couldn't hear. Both men looked toward the prison.

Jake ducked. Instinctively.

When he rose again, Orvis was gone. The supplies were in a pile.

And Rademacher was racing into Colonel Weymouth's tent. With the note.

He's giving it to Weymouth.

Which meant he wasn't the spy.

Which meant there was a chance of victory.

"Everybody! Out!" Orvis's voice, high-pitched and hysterical, rang through the cabin. "All men to fight! Corporal Rademacher say we needing all we have!"

"YEEEE-HAH!" Jamie hollered.

Yes.

Finally.

Jake's hands clenched. His throat constricted.

No retreating now, the way we did at Hobson's Corner.

This would be different.

This would be revenge.

This would be real.

Orvis fumbled with a set of keys, then inserted one into the cell door and turned.

Clarence abruptly kicked open the door. "Come on, Jamie!"

With a cry of surprise, Orvis flew across the room, slamming into the wall.

Jake ran to help him. "Are you okay?"

"Orvis not spy!" Orvis blurted out. "What Orvis tell you — South-North not matter — not means Orvis Rebel. Just needing job — "

"Don't worry!" Jake locked his arms around Orvis's shoulders and helped him outside. "We're even! I'm not a spy, either — "

"Orvis knows this. Rademacher tells. He says you smarter than you look. NO, NOT GO THIS WAY. TO LEFT!"

Orvis yanked Jake to the left. Pulled him to the ground.

BLAAAAAAM!

The ground erupted just to their right.

Clods of dirt rained around them. Jake rolled away and looked up.

Orvis was fine. But a crater had opened in the soil exactly where they'd been headed.

That could have been us.

Jake was shaking. The sound of the blast rang in his ears. H-h-how did you know?"

"I — I —" Orvis just shrugged.

"YEEEAAAAAAAGHHHH!"

A soldier was running toward Jake now, weaving. Shrieking.

The cook.

His eyes were wide, his head back. Blood dripped from a stump where his hand once was. It spurted as he pointed to Jake and Orvis. Then his face suddenly calmed and he began laughing uncontrollably.

"Down!" Orvis shouted. "He got the crazies! He — "

CRRRRRACK!

The cook's body lurched off the ground. He fell, staring at Jake, trying to utter a sound. Then his eyes rolled back into his head.

"NO-O-O-O-O!"

Real that was real it couldn't have been a

fake, the stump HOW DO YOU FAKE A STUMP? He's dead dead dead

Orvis was pulling Jake now. "Come!" he shouted. "Away from open fire!"

Suddenly Jake felt himself lifted off his feet. From behind.

"You!" Sergeant Edmonds yelled. "Say your prayers, 'cause you're a dead man."

"DEAD, THE COOK IS DEAD I SAW HIM — "

"I SHOULD THROW YOU TO YOUR OWN MEN!" Edmonds shouted. "YOU BE-TRAYED SAMUELSON. YOU GAVE UP THE CAMP — "

BLAAMMM!

Jake hurtled toward a long mortar-and-stone wall. He fell and rolled, with Edmonds and Orvis beside him. A line of soldiers was firing at the ridge, nestling their muskets between the stones.

Get away, you DON'T belong here, it's NOT better, it STINKS, go home go home NOW

Jake stood up.

CRRRACKKK!

"GET DOWN! ARE YOU NUTS?" Sergeant Edmonds bellowed.

Yes. Yes, THAT'S EXACTLY WHAT I AM —

"I — I have to go!" Jake said.

Edmonds shoved a musket in his hands. "TAKE THIS AND USE IT, OR GIVE IT TO ME AND I'LL SHOOT YOU RIGHT NOW!"

NO. NO!

"SERGEANT, I'M ONLY FOURTEEN — "

"Sergeant . . . "

Samuelson's voice.

Samuelson?

"You fool!" Edmonds shouted. "What are you doing out of the cabin?"

Samuelson crawled toward them, smiling weakly. "I heard you needed all the help you could get."

"There he is," Edmonds said, gesturing to Jake. "Judas. Kill him."

"S-s-sergeant, this is a big mistake," Jake stammered.

"He didn't betray me," Samuelson said. "He saved my life."

BOOOOM!

Stones and soil flew upward. Fifty yards away, a gap opened in the wall.

Closer, it's getting closer, the next one'll be here, time out, can we call a time-out —

"SHOOT, BRANFORD!"

Edmonds shoved Jake on his stomach. Propped the musket in a gap between the stones.

Jake looked through the sight. At a line of Rebels on the ridge.

Like my journal. Like the gray line I mowed down and it felt so good, so CLEAN and so EASY and here I am looking at them and they want to kill me.

One of the Rebels was aiming at him.

The trigger.

SQUEEZE THE TRIGGER!

KA-BLAM!

"AAAAAAAAAGH!" Jake recoiled.

A body was falling. Over the ridge. Screaming. Leaving a trail of bright red.

Did I do that?

I did.

I KILLED HIM.

It didn't feel good. Not at all. Jake wanted to throw up. The ground was whirling . . .

"I got him for you," Samuelson said. "You have to pull the trigger harder, son."

Suddenly Edmonds bellowed, "Cover the colonel!"

Steady.

Stay alive, Jake.

Breathe deep. See this through.

Jake glanced toward Colonel Weymouth's tent.

A squadron emerged. In formation. A V-shape like a flock of geese, with one man at the front and the others fanning out in back.

Briskly they walked forward, their muskets trained on the enemy, bursts of smoke puffing up with each shot fired.

In the midst of the formation, huddled together, were Colonel Weymouth and Mrs. Stoughton.

"What are they doing?" Jake asked.

"Weymouth insisted!" Edmonds shouted. "He wants to save her, at all costs. Now. In case they surround us. In case we're slaughtered. He thinks they won't fire on a woman — "

"He crazy!" Orvis said.

"He figures she can escape through the ravine while we focus fire on the rebels." Edmonds replied.

"What? He's using the men as a shield!" Jake said.

Edmonds didn't answer. But his eyes were a soldier's: they said *I obey; I don't question*.

The formation was moving. Slowly. Toward the woods.

This is the dumbest thing I have ever seen.

Union shots echoed. Rebel bodies fell from the ridge.

But the men in the formation were untouched. Unfired upon. All of them.

Jake stared in total disbelief.

Then a sudden, unexpected motion. Mrs. Stoughton, stumbling over her dress.

Colonel Weymouth pulled her arm. Hard.

She lunged forward and fell. Her purse fell to the ground, spilling its contents.

Jake's eyes fixed on one item.

A green piece of paper.

Quickly Weymouth stooped over. He picked up the paper.

For a moment he was exposed. An easy target.

But not one shot was fired near him.

Weymouth quickly stuffed the paper back into Mrs. Stoughton's purse. And he fell into position again, protected by the V.

It can't be.

They're leaving the camp.

With the plan.

But why?

Where would she be taking it?

The answer hit Jake over the head.

Hard.

"She — she — " Jake swallowed hard. "SHE HAS IT! SHE HAS THE PLAN!"

"What plan?" Edmonds shot back.

"Colonel Weymouth — didn't he tell — Rademacher knows about it!"

"Rademacher's dead! Someone shot him. In Weymouth's tent."

"What?"

"Sniper. The bullet must have gone right through the tent."

No. That wasn't it. The killer was inside.

"Who else was in there with him?" Jake asked.

"Just Colonel Weymouth and Mrs. Stoughton."

Jake glanced back at the woods.

The men had reached the tree line. In moments they'd be out of sight.

He's getting away with it.

The boy is on his own.

13

"STOP THEM!" Jake shouted as loud as he could. "THEY'RE THE SPIES! COLONEL WEYMOUTH AND MRS. STOUGHTON!"

"Whaaaat?" Samuelson said.

"That's treason!" Edmonds shot back.

Pull it together, Jake.

Make sense.

"Listen to me!" Jake persisted. "The Rebels have gone around us. They're squeezing us from two sides. I have a plan. We fight them off during the day and spread into the mountain passes at night. We counterattack. I wrote it all out. Rademacher took the plan to Colonel Weymouth. Then — *BAM* — he's killed mysteriously and Mrs. Stoughton is carrying the plan with her into the woods. *And the Rebels aren't shooting at them.* Put two and two together!"

"By god, it makes some kind of crazy sense," Samuelson said.

Edmonds's angry expression slackened.

"You have to believe me!" Jake insisted. "We can't let them go!"

"Colonel Weymouth?" muttered Edmonds, shaking his head. "Of all people, I never thought — "

"What do we do?" Samuelson asked.

"Follow them — now," Jake insisted. "The Rebels won't dare shoot at us for fear of killing the spies."

Edmonds glanced out to the moving V. "But once those men get into the woods . . ."

"Weymouth'll lead them into a trap," Jake said. "Somewhere."

Edmonds sprang upward and leaped over the stone wall. "ABANDON YOUR POSTS! FOLLOW THEM!"

"Jake, you're a genius!" Samuelson said, leaping up.

"What are you doing?" Jake said. "You were shot!"

"Never felt better!" Samuelson grabbed Jake by the arm.

The two of them ran after Edmonds.

A shot rang out. The ground erupted inches in front of them.

The open field.

Suicide.

THINK.

DON'T DIE.

Take cover along the way. Anywhere.

Jake made a break for the supply cabin. "Come on!" he called over his shoulder.

"NO! NOT THERE!"

Samuelson grabbed Jake from behind, flung him to the ground, and dove on top of him.

BOOOOOM!

The cabin erupted in a ball of fire.

Jake scrambled away, staring aghast at the flames.

He hadn't seen the cannonball.

Thank god Samuelson did.

"Come on!" Samuelson was yanking him upward.

He ran toward the V formation. Jake followed close behind.

Open field again.

"Go exactly where I go!" Samuelson cried out.

Jake didn't question.

Zig left.

Clods of dirt shot up from the ground to the right.

Zag right.

To their left, bullets shredded an empty tent.

My flesh, that could have been my chest, my arm, my face—

Some of Edmonds's men were charging forward, running flat out, on foot and on horses, pausing only to shoot toward the ridge.

Where are the rest of them?

Jake glanced over his shoulder. Toward the stone wall.

There they were. Mutineers. Doubters.

WHAAAAAAM!

The wall burst upward in a sudden geyser of rock, dirt, and smoke.

No.

Jake's heart skipped.

Dead.

All of them.

I would have been, too. And Samuelson. And Sergeant Edmonds.

If I hadn't convinced them.

"MOVE, BRANFORD!" Edmonds shouted.

Jake turned toward the woods.

Just ahead of them now, the last of Weymouth's V formation was climbing the hill.

Edmonds fired into the air. "Stop there!" he yelled.

Weymouth's men turned, muskets at the ready.

Expecting Rebels.

Their faces registered surprise. Disbelief.

Weymouth locked eyes with Edmonds.

"THE COLONEL IS A TRAITOR!" Edmonds announced.

Weymouth's face turned crimson. His upper lip curled back in anger. "Shoot to kill!" he commanded.

His soldiers gripped their guns. But no one fired.

"SHOOT, I SAY!" Weymouth roared.

Crrrack!

A flash of light.

The man to Jake's left vaulted off the ground. He fell in a motionless heap, his chest a red, wet mass of shredded material.

Oh no oh no no no NO NO

"GET DOWN!" Edmonds yelled.

Hide.

Jake dived. Rolled behind a tree. Curled up.

CRRRACK!

A body thumped to the ground beside him. Writhing. Kicking. Shrieking.

Edmonds.

"SERGEA-A-A-NT!" Jake cried.

"Chhh — gk — " Edmonds was trying to say something. His eyes were desperate, pleading.

Stop STOP STOP — DIE. PLEASE.

With a sudden choking sound, Edmonds went still.

Eyes still open. Still staring at Jake.

Jake heaved and puked. Without feeling much of anything.

Run.

His body was acting on its own now. His brain was separating. Deadening. He was fleeing. Through the woods.

Past a man who was bent over a tree.

Past Mrs. Stoughton, who was firing a pistol.

Past Weymouth's men fighting Edmonds's. Weymouth's fighting Weymouth's. A civil war within a civil war within a civil war.

The smell of gunpowder seared his lungs. The splinters from bullet-riddled trees nested in his hair.

And none of it meant a thing.

His musket was long gone. Dropped somewhere by the destroyed supply cabin.

But he had no desire to use it.

Killing didn't matter now.

Nothing mattered.

Nothing but his life.

There.

An opening.

He veered toward a clearing. A barely detectable path through the undergrowth.

"NO! NOT THAT WAY!" cried a voice behind him.

Don't listen.

In the distance, maybe fifty yards away, an object.

A building.

Yes. Go. Hide.

"STOP THERE OR YOU'RE DEAD!"

It was Weymouth's voice.

Right behind him.

Jake stopped.

And turned.

And froze.

Weymouth stood a few yards away. Glaring at Jake down the barrel of a musket. "We were so close to escape . . . so close."

Over. Done. The end.

Jake put his hands in the air. "You win," he said. "That's how this ends. You escape and no one ever finds out about you. I know."

Weymouth faltered a moment. Lowered the gun.

And in that moment, it all became clear to Jake. Weymouth the commander, Weymouth the powerful, was nothing. A blot in a history book, no more, no less.

"The funny thing is," Jake went on, "in the end, the battle means nothing. The war ends, and guess what? Your side loses anyway, Colonel. So everything you've done — the stolen plan, the escape, the deaths you just caused — what was the point?"

"No, my boy." Weymouth's face flushed. His eyes narrowed. "No one would have died just now if you had shut your mouth. Tactical error, soldier. A fatal one."

He raised the gun. Took aim.

"Wait," Jake said, backing away. "WAIT!"

Weymouth cocked the gun.

And fired.

14

AAAGH!"

Jake hit the ground.

He coughed. The dirt was sour on his tongue, the root had scratched his cheek, and the smoke hung heavy and acrid in the air.

Taste. Touch. Smell.

I'm alive.

Run.

Don't look back.

Jake scrambled to his feet and took off.

"HEY!"

Go.

He missed once. He won't do it again.

He raced toward the clearing.

The building.

Visible now. Through the branches.

A hut. Like the one Jake had seen the day before at the ridge.

"NOT THERE!"

BLAMMMMM!

Jake dived again. Blindly.

"GO LEFT!"

Weymouth was right behind him.

Think.

Jake darted to the right.

"I SAID NOT THAT WAY!"

Motion.

Near the hut. A figure in the shadows.

Human.

Weymouth's Confederate pals. Gathering for the ambush.

Forget the hut.

Only one direction remained.

Straight up the mountain.

Behind him, footsteps crashed through the underbrush. More than just Weymouth now.

"Stop!"

"You can't go there!"

"Get him!"

Voices. Lots of them.

You'll be in the crossfire.

GO!

Jake veered away.

Sprinted. Toward the base of the mountain.

Away from the voices. Away from the madness and the killing and the blood and the guilt —

Jake lurched downward.

Something was wrapped around his ankle.

He sprawled on the ground. Spun around. Sat up.

Reached down.

It wasn't a root.

It was long and black. Plastic.

A cable.

What the — ?

No time to think.

He could see them out of the corner of his eye.

Advancing through the woods toward him.

Weymouth. Soldiers. Mrs. Stoughton.

Go!

Jake stood up and ran.

The ankle throbbed. But it wasn't broken.

Ignore it.

Just. Go.

A voice was shouting something behind him.

Loud. Unnaturally loud. Magnified.

The echo of the mountain.

Jake began to climb. He planted his left foot and pulled himself upward on a branch. Then his right —

"OWWW!"

The ankle buckled. Jake fell.

He couldn't move.

Pain shot through him. Sharp. Blinding.

They were coming nearer now.

Weymouth was running up the mountain-side. Panting.

This is it.

Death.

A century and a quarter before your own birth.

And you can't do a thing about it.

What was the point, Jake?

Was this what you wanted?

The fighting, the blood, the death—was this the feeling?

Was it?

He gritted his teeth. Turned away.

"Hello?" Weymouth said. "Didn't you hear what he said?"

Jake peeked. Weymouth was giving him a peculiar look. His gun was at his side. He turned briefly and waved the other men off.

"What — who — ?" Jake stammered.

"Didn't you hear Mr. Kozaar? Through the loudspeaker?" Weymouth asked. "He yelled 'Cut!' "

Found him.

15

Cut?

Behind Colonel Weymouth, soldiers were now crowding the woods. Some were staring quizzically at Jake.

Others were cleaning their muskets.

Stretching. Laughing.

Cut?

In the distance, two familiar figures emerged from among the trees. The man on the left had a large red stain on his chest. The one on the right had what seemed to be a hole through his head.

Edmonds. Rademacher.

Cut?

Jake sank back in the brush. The scene seemed to whirl before him, and he felt as if he were floating.

A movie.

A man dressed in black was fixing Mrs. Stoughton's makeup. He was wearing a baseball cap embroidered with the words *Civil Disobedience*.

Behind him, a woman was bending over the wire Jake had stumbled over. "Affirmative on electrical damage," she called into a wireless headphone. "Send Herb after he fixes that memory chip."

The blood.

The deaths.

Fake.

All of it.

But how — ?

Jake's mind raced back over the last twenty-four hours — all the shootings and the bombings.

I never saw them. I never saw the bombs or the bullets. Just the aftermath.

The stone wall. The massacre of Edmonds's men.

Rigged.

The exploding munitions cabin.

Choreographed.

That was why Edmonds pulled me away before it happened. He knew in advance.

"Nice job, kid."

Edmonds.

No, that's not his name. He's an actor.

"Almost lost you there," the actor said. "What's the matter, couldn't find your scene map?"

"Scene map?" Jake asked.

The man's face fell. "Didn't they give you one?"

No. They didn't.

He didn't.

Gideon Kozaar.

Jake looked past Edmonds. Past the chattering actors, the occasional puffs of cigarette smoke, the dead men come to life.

Beyond them was the hut.

Lopsided, boarded up.

Its door opened briefly. And Jake saw, silhouetted in deep red light, the profile of a man wearing earphones.

Jake stood slowly. Pain shot upward from his ankle.

He hobbled a few steps, then steadied.

"Kid? Are you okay?"

Jake ignored the question. He elbowed his way through the crowd until he reached the hut.

The door was padlocked.

He grabbed the lock and pulled anyway.

The door swung open.

In the red light, the room seemed bathed in blood. Along one wall, a bank of monitors glowed dully with familiar images: the encampment, the woods, the ridge, the hut itself from the other side.

"I was wondering when you'd find me." Gideon Kozaar's back was to Jake. He was staring at the monitors.

"This is — this is so — " Jake spluttered.

"Unfair?" Kozaar turned. A small, tight smile played beneath his beard.

"I could have been killed!"

"Not likely. The cast was well trained to protect you. They knew where the explosives were. They were equipped with hidden earphones that warned them of the timing. Some got carried away. James Nickerson — the fellow who plays Rademacher — he will be fined for what he did to your cheek. And if you need plastic surgery, I will pay for it. But this is the price for art, Jake. Not every fourteen-year-old stars in a movie based on himself."

"Based on *me*? You don't know me!"

"I didn't have to know you. You created the story as I watched — the tale of a war-loving boy named Jake who wills himself into the past and finds what war is really like."

"How — how did you do it? The old village — ?"

"A replica. Built by my construction crew. They cleared a spot in the woods, even landscaped the soil. You met three of them on the day I gave you the note. They were checking the topography of your neighborhood, fine-tuning. Impressive, eh?"

"What if I hadn't found the set? I nearly didn't — "

"I had faith."

" — And where were you when I got there? Why didn't you *tell* me it was a movie?"

"It would have made you self-conscious. If you knew it was a film, you never would have given the powerful performance you did."

Powerful?

I gave up.

I ran.

I was weak.

And the world is going to see it.

"No — " Jake murmured.

"Bravery versus prudence," Kozaar said. "Arrogance versus humility. Tactics gone wrong. Life and death. All wrapped up in a nifty whodunit. You'll be instant A-list in Hollywood."

"I don't care about that! You can't show this!"

"Oh? Don't like what you saw? Shall we re-shoot?"

No.

Never.

Never in a million years.

Don't listen to him.

"I — I need to go," Jake said. "My brother is probably freaking out."

"He knows," Gideon Kozaar replied with a shrug. "I told him. And he gave me your parents' number in Chicago. They're very proud of you. I believe your mother's exact words were, 'He's in his element.' And I must agree. Although I was a bit surprised by how you chose to end it — "

"I didn't choose anything! I just — "

" — But that's the beauty of improvisation. You never know what will happen, do you? Even if you think you will. Even if you've been there a thousand times in your mind. At home. Tucked away in your private world."

Gideon Kozaar smiled, and Jake felt as if he'd been scratched by an icepick.

Kozaar's eyes seemed to shift color and depth, a dark pit giving way to an endless sky, a flame turning to frost.

He knew.

Everything.

He's seen me in the attic. He's read the journal. Reached into my thoughts.

But how?

"Who . . . are . . . you?" Jake asked.

"The same as you, Jake. Only you don't know it yet."

"What's that supposed to mean?"

"You'll find out, if you're ready. And if you

do, think of me. I may be long gone. I wasn't supposed to tell you even this much, and I may suffer for it." Kozaar sighed. "But I never was much for following rules. It's only by breaking them that progress is made, don't you think? Sometimes the rebels actually win. Now, if you'll excuse me . . ."

Turning abruptly, Kozaar headed for the door on the other side.

"Wait!" Jake shouted.

Over his head, he spotted movement on one of the monitors. A view from an outside camera. The camera that was trained on the hut.

As Kozaar opened the door, the door in the image opened.

As Kozaar stepped out and shut the door behind him, the door in the image slammed shut, too.

But no one passed through.

"What the — ?"

Jake ran to the door and flung it open.

Before him, a table of food was being laid out for the actors and crew. As Jake scanned the area, he noticed things he hadn't seen before — mikes, speakers, cameras — tiny black objects, hidden in the trees and bushes. Some were wireless, some attached to cords.

Were they there before?

How could I have missed them?

Jake still had a million questions.

But Gideon Kozaar was gone.

We have him in our sights now.

But the boy — he knows.

Can we bring him back?

I don't believe this. He's on his way.

But the *boy*. He's the only one who's ever made contact.

He broke the rules again. He must be expelled.

No Watcher has ever been —

But what about the boy?

16

"I should have broken character. What a jerk I was. Can you ever forgive me?"

James Nickerson sat at the edge of the Branfords' living room sofa. His red hair was swept back, moussed. His chin was smooth, the grime gone from his face. His skin was bright red — because of embarrassment this time, not anger.

Jake gently fingered the cut on his cheek. It was still sore and the scab was starting to harden. "It'll heal."

"I would have backed off," Byron murmured sullenly. "If he'd have hired me."

"You know what Kozaar told us?" Nickerson hunched his shoulders and lowered his voice to a pitch-perfect imitation: " 'You may not act. You must *be* your character until I say "Cut," and not a moment before — whether it takes an afternoon, a day, a week.' All we know is that a kid is coming, and we have to do two things: react to whatever he does and protect him from the explosives. Plus, when the kid says he wants to go home, we have to take him to the Hobson's Corner set. We have these little chips behind our ears for whenever Kozaar needs to direct us — which is practically never."

"I don't get how he builds a whole village that no one knows about," Byron grumbled.

"The cops knew," Nickerson said. "The Hobson's Corner Chamber of Commerce. The local government. They made sure no planes flew overhead, stuff like that — and they were sworn to secrecy. Anyway, so we're in this camp, this huge outdoor set. The cameras and mikes are hidden away — everything's wireless — and it's magic. Like we're *in* the war. But it doesn't take an afternoon or even a week. Two weeks go by before Jake actually shows up."

"And you just *stayed*?" Byron asked.

"No choice. We're pros. We can't bathe or brush our teeth or watch TV or say anything our characters wouldn't say. But the weird thing is — no one complains. Because we're not ourselves anymore. Slowly we've *become* the characters. Only they're not characters. Not really." Nickerson's face darkened. "They're parts of ourselves. Hidden inside. Parts we maybe don't know about. Maybe for good reason. So . . . what I'm trying to say is, I'm sorry about what I did. Jake was the one who showed courage."

Courage.

Jake didn't know what the word meant anymore.

At this point he just knew what it *didn't* mean.

It didn't mean strategy. Or tactics. Or arms or training.

In the end, none of that mattered.

All of it was as fragile as a thought.

In the end, you were left with only chaos.

And death.

Unless you're lucky, and it's all a fake.

After Jake said good-bye to James Nickerson, he walked upstairs. Into the attic.

He felt for the green steno journal in his back pocket.

It was there, but the urge to write wasn't.

The mood — *the feeling* — was gone.

Only numbness was left.

Numbness and confusion.

Jake flicked on the antique lamp and sat by the steamer trunk. A mournful sadness settled over him. In the excitement and horror of the movie shoot, he'd forgotten to ask about his cap and the uniform.

Too late now. Gideon Kozaar had disappeared. A check had already arrived to cover the cost of the "antiques." No return address.

Jake yanked open the old trunk. The moldy sweet smell of the past wafted upward.

What?

There, on top of the pile of clothes, was a Civil War uniform.

And a cap.

And a dagger.

Jake smiled.

Feverishly he dug his hands under the clothing and pulled on the handle of the secret compartment.

Inside was a book. Crumbling and brittle. Held together by a faded satin cord.

Jake carefully took it out. It was some kind of scrapbook, stuffed to the brim with photos, letters, and newspaper clippings.

On the soft cloth cover he could feel an embroidered inscription.

He held it to the light and read:

IN MEMORIAM
Jedidiah
Samuelson
1845—1930

Jake opened the book and quickly leafed through . . . photos, news clippings, pages from a personal journal . . .

There.

Under the heading "The Battle of Dead Man's Trace":

I still find it difficult to fathom the events of that fateful day. Of the battle that we almost certainly would have lost, but for the actions of a young soldier I shall not soon forget . . .

Jake looked around the attic.
No cameras.
Hesitantly, he continued to read.

WATCHERS
Case file: 6955

Name: Jacob Branford

Age: 14

First contact: 57.34.43

Acceptance: YES

Marion Etlinger

ABOUT THE AUTHOR

Peter Lerangis is the author of more than one hundred books, including two Young Adult thrillers, *The Yearbook* and *Driver's Dead*. He was once a stage actor, which often allowed him to travel into the past. He still enjoys doing it as an author, although he misses the costumes. Mr. Lerangis lives in New York City with his wife, Tina deVaron, and his two sons, Nick and Joe.